Winnie-the-Pooh
CHRISTMAS
STORIES

EGMONT

Contents

- page 9 -

Pooh's Snowy Day

in which a house is built at Pooh Corner for Eeyore

- page 37 -

Pooh's Christmas Adventure

in which Pooh and his friends get snowed in

- page 63 -

Pooh's Christmas Letters

in which Pooh's friends are invited to the North Pole

Winnie-the-Pooh

Pooh's Snowy Day

One morning Pooh wasn't doing very much, so he thought he would go and visit Piglet. But when he got to Piglet's house, Piglet wasn't there. Bother, thought Pooh to himself, and he decided to go back home.

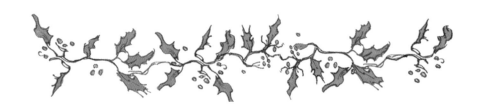

When Pooh got back to his own house, he found Piglet sitting in his best armchair. For a moment he wondered whose house he was in.

"Hello Piglet," he said. "I thought you were out."

"No," said Piglet. "It's you who were out, Pooh!"

When they had had a little something to eat,
Pooh and Piglet decided to visit Eeyore.
On the way they sang a special outdoor song that
Pooh had written:

"The more it snows, Tiddley Pom!" it went.

By this time Pooh and Piglet were close to where Eeyore lived.

"I've been thinking," said Pooh. "Eeyore's place is very gloomy. Why don't we build him a new house?"

"I saw a heap of sticks on the other side of the wood," said Piglet, helpfully.

"Let's go and fetch them," said Pooh, "and build a house here."

A little bit later, Christopher Robin was just about to go outside when who should arrive at his front door but Eeyore.

"Hello Christopher Robin," said Eeyore. "I don't suppose you've seen my house anywhere, have you?"

"Your house?" said Christopher Robin.

"It gets very cold on my side of the forest," explained Eeyore. "So I built myself a little house to keep warm in, and I went back there this morning, and IT'S GONE!"

"Oh, Eeyore," said Christopher Robin.

Eeyore and Christopher Robin set off together to look for Eeyore's little house.

"There!" said Eeyore, "You see. Not a stick of it left!"

But Christopher Robin wasn't listening. In the distance he could hear . . . what was it?

Christopher Robin moved closer to where
the strange sound was coming from. It sounded
like two voices singing—first a gruff one and then
a higher, squeakier one.

"It's Pooh and Piglet!" said Christopher Robin.

Sure enough, there were Pooh and Piglet coming toward them.

"There's Christopher Robin!" squeaked Piglet.

"He's over by the place where we found all those sticks!"

After Christopher Robin had given Pooh a hug, he told Pooh and Piglet about the sad story of Eeyore's lost house. And the more he talked, the more Pooh and Piglet's eyes seemed to get bigger and bigger.

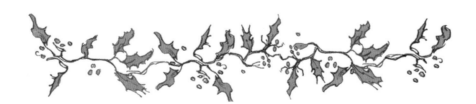

"The fact is . . ." said Pooh. "Well, the fact is . . ."

"It's like this," said Piglet ". . . only WARMER."

"What's warmer?" asked Christopher Robin.

"The other side of the wood, where Eeyore's house is," said Piglet. "We'll show you," said Pooh.

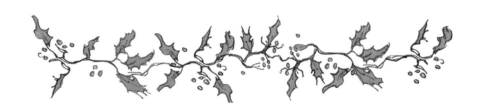

So they went over to the other side of the forest, and sure enough there was Eeyore's house.

"It IS my house," said Eeyore. "And I built it where I said I did. The wind must have blown it here." And Eeyore happily settled down in his new house.

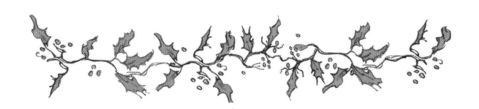

Pooh, Piglet and Christopher Robin went back home to lunch, and on the way Pooh and Piglet told him about the Awful Mistake they had made. Christopher Robin just laughed, and they all sang Pooh's song all the way home.

Tiddley Pom! Tiddley Pom!

Winnie-the-Pooh

Pooh's Christmas Adventure

It was a cold, snowy day in the Hundred Acre Wood. Winnie-the-Pooh watched the snowflakes fall outside his window.

"I love it when it snows," Pooh said. "But it makes me so very hungry."

Pooh decided to have his favourite snack – honey.

When Pooh finished eating, he looked out of the window again. Now all he could see was white. *Oh dear,* he thought. *Something is wrong with the windows.* But soon he realised he was snowed in.

"What shall I do?" he wondered.

After much thinking, Pooh had an idea.

He could use his honey-pot to dig himself out.

"All this work is making me rather hungry,"
Pooh said as he tunnelled through the snow.
"But I've run out of honey. Perhaps Piglet has some."

Pooh arrived at Piglet's house and found him snowed in, too. So Pooh used the honey-pot to dig out his friend. It took him quite a bit of time.

"Thank you," Piglet cried when Pooh finally reached Piglet's door. "You rescued me!"

"It's ... no ... bother ..." puffed Pooh, trying to catch his breath. "Do you have any honey?"

"I'm afraid not," Piglet said. "But Owl might!"

Pooh and Piglet walked to Owl's house and found that he was snowed in too.

"I suppose I'll have to dig again," Pooh sighed.

"It will be easier if we dig together," Piglet suggested.

"What a grand idea!" said Pooh.

Pooh and Piglet worked together to dig out Owl.
This time, the digging went much more quickly.
"Thank you," Owl said as he opened his door.
"Would you like some hot tea?"
"With honey?" Pooh asked hopefully.

47

After warming up inside Owl's house, the three friends went to dig out Rabbit. Things were going quite well until they heard a scratching sound.

"Whatever could that be?" Pooh asked.

"P-p-perhaps it is a Heffalump!" Piglet cried.

Suddenly Rabbit burst through the snow!
"What are you doing here?" Rabbit cried.
"We're here to dig you out," Piglet said.

"But I was coming to dig you out," Rabbit said.
"Rabbits are natural diggers, you know."

"Well, perhaps we ought to go and dig Eeyore
out," Owl suggested. "With all four of us, it should take
no time at all."

So Pooh, Piglet, Owl and Rabbit went to Eeyore's house.

Everyone helped with the digging, and they uncovered Eeyore's house in no time.

Pooh tugged on the bell rope to let Eeyore know they were there, but it made a very peculiar sound: "Ow!"

"If I'm not mistaken," Rabbit began, "I'd say that's not a bell rope, it's Eeyore's tail!"

"I'm terribly sorry," said Pooh.

"Don't worry," Eeyore sighed. "No one bothers about me anyway."

"But, Eeyore," Piglet explained, "we've just rescued you!"

"And now that you've been rescued, let's see if Christopher Robin needs our help," Owl said.

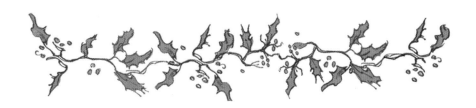

Pooh, Piglet, Owl, Rabbit and Eeyore came upon Christopher Robin in the forest.

"Are you stuck? Shall we help dig you out?" asked Pooh. "We're really quite good at it."

"I'm not stuck, you silly old Bear!" laughed Christopher Robin. "I'm making a snowman!"

"A snowman?" Pooh asked curiously. "How do you make one of those?"

"I'll show you," Christopher Robin said. "If we all work together, it'll be an even better one!"

So Christopher Robin, Pooh and Rabbit helped to roll a giant snowball for the snowman's body. Eeyore found stones to use for the snowman's face. Piglet searched for twigs to use as arms, and Owl flew them into place.

"This is the grandest snowman I've ever seen!" Christopher Robin said. "And I couldn't have done it without all of you!"

Winnie-the-Pooh

Pooh's Christmas Letters

One cold morning, Pooh was strolling through the Hundred Acre Wood ...

. . . and humming
a little hum to himself
when he had an idea.
It was a good idea.
A CHRISTMASSY idea.

The next morning Piglet woke up to find a letter on his doorstep.

"Please come to the North Pole at lunchtime.

Signed, a Friend," it said.

Piglet was confused. Who could have written it?

Piglet decided to take the letter to Pooh.
Even though Pooh was a Bear of Very Little
Brain, he might know who had written it.

But when Piglet got to Pooh's house, Pooh wasn't there. "Hello Piglet," said Christopher Robin, stomping through the snow in his wellington boots. "Where's Winnie-the-Pooh?"

Piglet explained that he didn't know. "I've had a letter, Christopher Robin," he said.

"May I see it, please?" asked Christopher Robin. After he had read it he thought for a moment and said, "I'd better go to the North Pole. You fetch the others, Piglet, and meet me there . . ."

Piglet went straight to Kanga's house. They had had a letter too!
"Merry Christmas," it said.
"Come to the North Pole for lunch.
A Friend."

Tigger and Roo were very excited. They couldn't wait to get going. But Kanga was cautious. "Let's go and see Rabbit – he always knows what to do," she said.

On the other side of the forest, Eeyore and Owl had also received a letter. "If you come to the North Pole I will reveal my surprise," it said. "Oh," said Eeyore gloomily, "I thought it might have been something important."

"Most curious," said Owl. "I believe we ought to consult Rabbit." And off they went, through the deep snow, to Rabbit's house.

They arrived at the same time as Kanga, Roo and Tigger. Rabbit was reading a letter that had come through his door that morning.

"Happy Christmas! Tiddley Pom!" he read. "Hurry to the North Pole for a surprise luncheon!"

"I believe," said Rabbit, "that if we go to the North Pole, we shall find out who has written these mysterious letters."

So they all set off through the crunchy snow to the North Pole. Rabbit led the way, and all the other friends followed behind him.

"I hope a HEFFALUMP didn't write the letters," said Piglet anxiously.

Soon they arrived at the North Pole, and there, waiting for them, were Christopher Robin and Winnie-the-Pooh! "Happy Christmas!" cried Pooh. "It was me who sent you all the letters! And there's one letter left."

Christopher Robin read the last letter aloud.
It was a Christmas card to all his friends.
"Welcome to my surprise Christmas Luncheon,"
it read. "There's plenty for everyone!"

And so they all sat down to eat their Christmas Lunch, organised by their dear friend, Pooh Bear. Everyone had a wonderful time – even Eyore!

EGMONT

We bring stories to life

First published in Great Britain 2014
by Egmont UK Limited, The Yellow Building, 1 Nicholas Road, London W11 4AN
www.egmont.co.uk

Illustrated by Andrew Grey
Based on the 'Winnie-the-Pooh' works by A.A.Milne and E.H.Shepard
Illustrations © 2014 Disney Enterprises Inc.

ISBN 978 1 4052 7295 7

A CIP catalogue record for this title is available from the British Library.

Stay safe online. Any website addresses listed in this book are correct at the time of going to print.
However, Egmont is not responsible for content hosted by third parties. Please be aware that
online content can be subject to change and websites can contain content that is unsuitable for
children. We advise that all children are supervised when using the internet.

Egmont is passionate about helping to preserve the world's remaining ancient forests.
We only use paper from legal and sustainable forest sources.

This book is made from paper certified by the Forest Stewardship Council® (FSC),
an organisation dedicated to promoting responsible management of forest resources.
For more information on the FSC, please visit www.fsc.org. To learn more about
Egmont's sustainable paper policy, please visit www.egmont.co.uk/ethical.